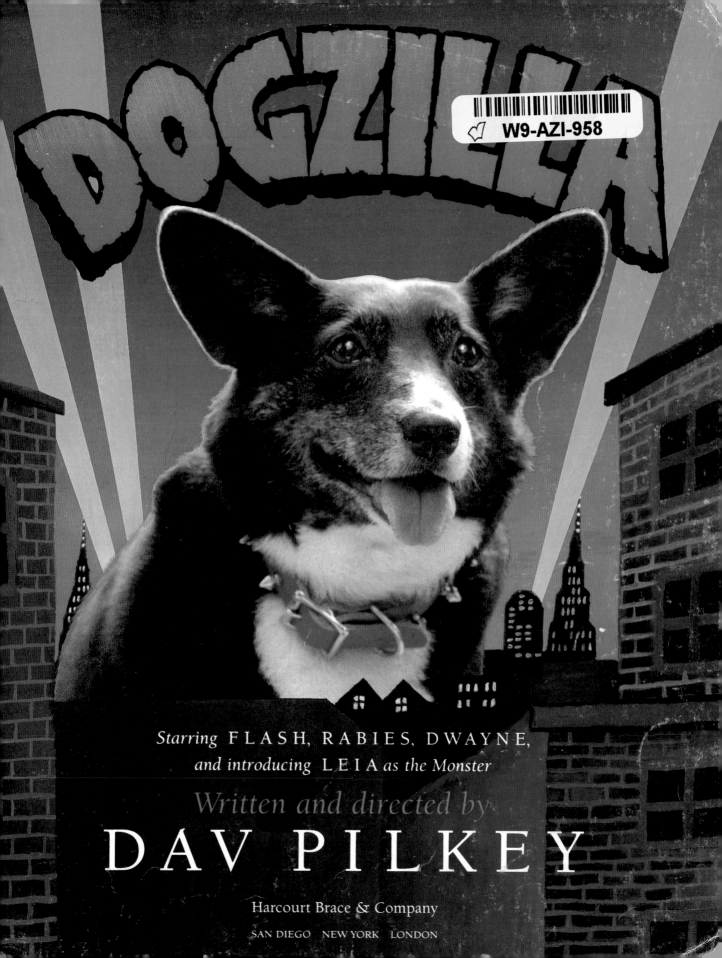

DOGZILLA

Starring FLASH, RABIES, DWAYNE,
and introducing LEIA as the Monster

Written and directed by

DAV PILKEY

Harcourt Brace & Company

SAN DIEGO   NEW YORK   LONDON

Special Edition for Scholastic Book Fairs, Inc.

A B C D E

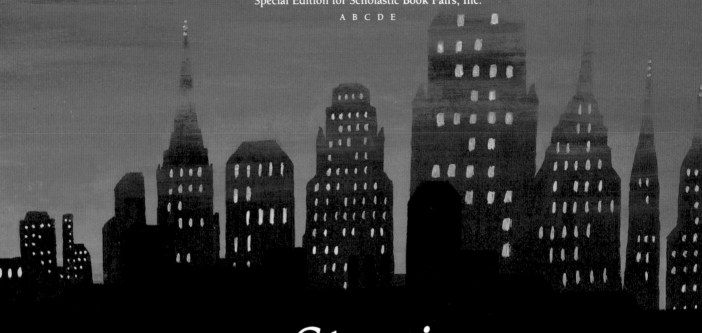

Starring

FLASH
as the Big Cheese

RABIES
*as Professor
Scarlett O'Hairy*

Special appearance by
DWAYNE
as the Soldier Guy

LEIA
as the Monster

The illustrations in this book are manipulated photographic collage,
heavily retouched with acrylic paint.

Special thanks to Kennebec Cardigan Welsh Corgis, Mentor, Ohio.

Printed in Singapore

For JOHN "The Rapper" WILLS

It was summertime in the city of Mousopolis,
and mice from all corners of the community

had come together to compete in the First Annual
Barbecue Cook-Off.

As the cook-off got under way, smoke from the hot grills lifted the irresistible scent of barbecue sauce over the rooftops of the city.

A gentle wind carried the mouth-watering smell into the

distance, right over the top of an ancient crater. Before long,
a strange and mysterious sound was heard: "Sniff . . . sniff.
Sniff . . . sniff sniff sniff sniff . . ."

All at once, the volcano began to tremble.

And suddenly, up from the very depths of the earth came the most

terrifying creature ever known to mousekind: the dreadful Dogzilla!

Immediately, soldiers were sent out to stop the mighty
beast. The heroic troops were led by their brave commanding
officer, the Big Cheese.

"All right, you old fleabag," squeaked the Big Cheese,
"get those paws in the air—you're coming with us!"

Without warning, the monstrous mutt breathed her horrible breath onto the mice.

"Doggy breath!" screamed the soldiers. "Run for your lives!"

"Hey, come back here," shouted the Big Cheese to his troops. "What are you, men or mice?"

"We're MICE," they squeaked.

"Hmmmm," said the Big Cheese, "you're *right!* . . . Wait for me!"

The colossal canine followed the soldiers back to Mousopolis,
licking up all of the food in her path.

Afterward, Dogzilla wandered through the city streets, doing those things that come naturally to dogs.

Dogzilla chased cars—right off the freeway!

Dogzilla chewed furniture—and the furniture store as well.

And Dogzilla dug up bones—

at the Museum of Natural History.

Meanwhile, the Big Cheese had organized an emergency meeting with one of the city's greatest scientific minds, Professor Scarlett O'Hairy.

"Gentlemice," said Professor O'Hairy, "this monster comes from prehistoric times. It is perhaps millions of years old."

"Maybe we could teach it to do something positive for the community," suggested the Big Cheese.

"I'm afraid not," said Professor O'Hairy. "You simply *can't* teach an old dog new tricks!

"If we're going to defeat this dog, we've got to *think* like a dog! We've got to find something that *all* dogs are afraid of—something that will scare this beast away from Mousopolis FOREVER!"

"I've got an idea," squeaked the Big Cheese . . .

Within minutes, the mice had assembled at the center
of town.

"All right, Dogzilla," shouted the Big Cheese, "no more Mister Mice Guy—it's BATHTIME!"

Suddenly, a blast of warm, sudsy water hit Dogzilla with tremendous force.

The panicking pooch let out a burst of hot, fiery breath, and the chase was on!

The Big Cheese tried to catch up to the hot dog

with all the relish he could muster.

Dogzilla hightailed it out of town, and back into the mouth
of the ancient volcano.

"Well, I'll be dog-goned," squeaked the Big Cheese.
"It worked!"

With the horrifying memory of the bubble bath etched in her mind forever, Dogzilla never again returned to Mousopolis.

Within a year, Mousopolis had rebuilt itself . . . just in time for the Second Annual Barbeque Cook-Off. The mice of Mousopolis fired up their grills, confident that they would never see or hear from Dogzilla again.

However, there was one thing they hadn't counted on . . .

Puppies!